KATIE MORAG and the BIG BOY COUSINS

High Farm

The Holiday House

Mrs Bayview's

The Lady

The Redburn Bridge

Effie & Ronald the Road's

The Village

Nurse's

Mrs Baxter's

Neilly Beag's

The Ferryman's

THE ISLE of STRUAY

Grannie's

The Mainland

The Jetty

ISLE of STRUAY
SHOP & POST OFFICE

OBAN
TIMES
GET
YOUR COPY
HERE

The Shop & Post Office

ALSO BY MAIRI HEDDERWICK IN RED FOX
Katie Morag and the New Pier
Katie Morag and the Two Grandmothers
Katie Morag and the Wedding
Katie Morag and the Riddles
Katie Morag and the Tiresome Ted
Katie Morag and the Grand Concert

A Red Fox Book
Published by Random House Children's Books
61-63 Uxbridge Road, London W5 5SA,

A division of The Random House Group Ltd
London Melbourne Sydney Auckland
Johannesburg and agencies throughout the world

7 9 8 10

First published in Great Britain by
The Bodley Head Children's Books 1987
Red Fox edition 1999

Printed in China
THE RANDOM HOUSE GROUP Ltd Reg. No. 954009
www.kidsatrandomhouse.co.uk

ISBN 0 09 911891 2
ISBN 978 0 099 11891 6 (from January 2007)

To all who cope with temptation

KATIE MORAG and the BIG BOY COUSINS

Mairi Hedderwick

RED FOX

It was the second fortnight in July, and Katie Morag's Big Boy Cousins had arrived from the Mainland to camp at Grannie Island's, as they did each summer.

"Oh, no!" sighed the islanders. "Here they come AGAIN!"
The Big Boy Cousins were very wild and unruly. Katie Morag thought they
were wonderful.

STRUAY LASS

THE TEAM

BULK BEANS

"Why do you put up with them, Grannie Island?" exclaimed Mr and Mrs McColl.

"Because nobody else will have them!" declared Grannie Island. "And I could do with some help with the chores."

Grannie Island loaded the provisions into her tractor and trailer, ready for the long, bumpy journey back to her house on the other side of the Bay. "Coming, Katie Morag?" smiled the biggest Boy Cousin called Hector.

BULK
MARSH
MALLOWS

Aug 1st
65th
Annual Show

EARLY
ENTRIES
PLEASE

Soon the tent was pitched and the stores unloaded.

"Now," called Grannie Island. "There are potatoes to be dug up, peats to be fetched and driftwood to be gathered. Who is doing what?"

THE
TEAM'S
BACK

MIDGE
REPELLENT

"GEE WHILICKERS!" groaned Hector, Archie, Dougal, Jamie and Murdo Iain.

Everyone pretended not to hear Grannie Island, even Katie Morag.

"Hide down by the shore!" whispered Hector.

"It's boring here," moaned Archie, after a while.
"We'll go to the Village, then, and play Chickenelly," said Hector.
"Yeah!" chorused all the Big Boy Cousins – except for Murdo Iain.
"It's an awful long walk," he whined.

"I know a quick way," chirped up Katie Morag.
She was enjoying being naughty and continued to ignore Grannie Island's cries for help.

In the Village all was calm and peaceful. The villagers were inside their houses, having a well-earned rest after a morning's hard work.

Nobody noticed Grannie Island's heavily laden boat, heading across the Bay.

Chickenelly was a daring game.

"Last one gets caught!" whispered Hector, as he led all the cousins on tiptoe round the gable end of Nurse's house.

Katie Morag's tummy tickled inside with excitement.

Then the Big Boy Cousins, with Katie Morag close on their heels, ran as fast as greased lightning, the length of the Village, banging very loudly on each back door.

BANG-a-BANG-a-BANG-a-BANG-a-BANG!

In their mad rush to get to the safety of the other end of the village houses, they knocked into all sorts of things, and nobody saw Grannie Island racing round the head of the Bay on her tractor.

ISLE of STRUAY
SHOP & POST OFFICE

"And just WHAT do you think you are all up to?" Grannie Island was colossal with fury.

"Chickenelly," said Katie Morag, timidly, wishing she had never heard of the game.

"Gee whilickers!" groaned Hector, Archie, Dougal, Jamie and Murdo Iain.

Grannie Island made them all apologize to the upset villagers and told them to clear up the mess they had caused.

"And you can all WALK back when you are finished!" she shouted.

Even though Grannie Island was angry outside, Katie Morag knew her Grannie was sad inside, and that made Katie Morag feel sad, too.

Tired and very hungry, the Big Boy Cousins were silent on the long journey
back to Grannie Island's.
Katie Morag walked as fast as she could.

"We've got to say sorry to Grannie," she said.
"*And* help her with the chores."
"Gee whilickers!" groaned Hector, Archie, Dougal,
Jamie *and* Murdo Iain.

The chores didn't take that long once everyone lent a hand. Katie Morag worked hardest of them all, and she made sure that the Big Boy Cousins didn't skive.

"Last chore!" called a smiling Grannie Island. "Bring over some of the potatoes, the peats and the driftwood."

Nobody groaned "Gee whilickers" this time. Grannie Island had made a barbecue.

"This is what I would call a hard-earned feast," said Grannie Island, dishing out mounds of fried tatties and beans.

"Tomorrow – " she continued – "*after* the chores, we'll go fishing and see what we can catch for another feast."

"*Not* chickenellies!" giggled Katie Morag.

And when it came to toasting the marshmallows, Katie Morag made sure Grannie Island got the biggest one.

That was fair, wasn't it?